D0272696

HORRID HENRY

ANNUAL 2020

HORRID HENRY

ANNUAL 2020

FRANCESCA SIMON
ILLUSTRATED BY TONY ROSS

Orion

ORION CHILDREN'S BOOKS

First published in Great Britain in 2019
by Hodder and Stoughton

1 3 5 7 9 10 8 6 4 2

This compilation, *Horrid Henry's Annual 2020* © Orion Children's Books 2019
Text © Francesca Simon 2019
Illustrations © Tony Ross 2019
Additional images © Shutterstock © Artful Doodlers

Compiled by Sally Byford from the *Horrid Henry* books
by Francesca Simon & illustrated by Tony Ross

The moral rights of the author and illustrator have been asserted.

A CIP catalogue record for this book
is available from the British Library.

ISBN 978 1 5101 0654 3

Printed and bound in Spain

The paper and board used in this book are from
well-managed forests and other responsible sources.

Orion Children's Books
An imprint of
Hachette Children's Group
Part of Hodder and Stoughton
Carmelite House
50 Victoria Embankment
London EC4Y 0DZ

An Hachette UK Company
www.hachette.co.uk
www.hachettechildrens.co.uk
www.horridhenry.co.uk

CONTENTS

Hello, Henry fans!
Calling all Purple
Hand Gang members!

Yo! Welcome to my biggest, baddest annual EVER!
Smelly toads keep away, and that includes any nappy
noodle mini ninnies like Peter.

If you've ever wanted to know how to defeat vicious
veg, or stop Nudie Foodies from tricking you into
eating healthy food instead of sweets and burgers
and crisps — well, you've come to the right place.
Chef Henry will be treating you to his favourite
gastronomic delights. If you can unwrap a chocolate
bar or microwave a pizza, you have all the skills you
need to work in my kitchen.

Who's the greatest?
Me, me and me!

Happy reading!

Henry

HENRY HAS
HIDDEN HIS BARS OF
CHOCOLATE AROUND
THE ANNUAL. HOW
MANY CAN YOU FIND?
THE ANSWER IS ON
PAGE 58.

MY FAMILY: WHO'S WHO

ME!

Lord High Excellent Majesty of the Family of Horrid Henry.

Leader of the Purple Hand Gang. Undiscovered genius.

PERFECT PETER

My little brother.

He likes TV programmes for babies, helping Mum and Dad with chores and doing his homework. Yeuch! What a slimy worm and a wibble pants.

MUM AND DAD

The most mean and miserable parents in the whole world. They like camping, hiking, vegetables and tiny TVs.

MOODY MARGARET

This grumpy, grouchy old frogface is my worst enemy ever! She's the leader of the puny Secret Club, and she loves bossing everyone around. If she doesn't get her own way, she SCREAMS!

BOSSY BILL

The slimy son of Dad's boss. He's a mean, double-crossing creep who tries to get me into trouble. And he's friends with the toadiest boy who ever slithered out of a swamp – my cousin, Stuck-Up Steve.

MISS BATTLE-AXE

The meanest teacher in the school. Why do I have to be in her class? It's not fair! She's always glaring at me with her beady eyes, and she gives out loads of horrible homework.

SOUR SUSAN

Moody Margaret's best friend, and Chief Spy for the Secret Club. Sour Susan likes sulking and telling tales. She falls out with Moody Margaret nearly every day because they are both sour old bossyboots.

13

BRAINY BRIAN'S BIG QUIZ

TUCK IN AND TRY YOUR LUCK!

1

WHY DOES PERFECT PETER THROW SPAGHETTI ALL OVER MUM?

a. He aimed at Henry – but Henry ducked!

b. He didn't want spaghetti – he wanted pizza.

c. Because Mum called him a wibble worm.

2

WHEN HORRID HENRY AND MOODY MARGARET MAKE GLOP, WHAT ARE THE TWO TOP INGREDIENTS?

a. Snails and worms.

b. Baked beans and peanut butter.

c. Cabbage and cauliflower.

Nice try Henry
The Tooth Fairy

3

HORRID HENRY IS DESPERATE TO GET SOME MONEY FROM THE TOOTH FAIRY. HOW DOES HE FINALLY LOSE A TOOTH?

a. By scoffing a mouthful of sticky sweets.

b. By biting into a crisp apple.

c. By munching on a big crunchy carrot.

4

HOW DOES HENRY DESTROY PRISSY POLLY AND PIMPLY PAUL'S WEDDING CAKE?

a. He knocks it off the table – whoops!

b. He throws it out of the window.

c. He eats a little bit – and then keeps eating, until a great big chunk is missing!

5

HORRID HENRY RUNS AWAY TO MOODY MARGARET'S TREEHOUSE. WHAT MAKES HIM GO HOME?

a. He smells pancakes, his favourite breakfast.

b. He's eaten all his running-away crisps and sweets.

c. He's eaten all of Moody Margaret's running-away biscuits.

6

WHEN HENRY AND HIS FAMILY DINE AT RESTAURANT LE POSH, WHAT DOES HENRY ORDER BY MISTAKE?

a. Beetroot mousse.

b. Squid in maggot sauce.

c. Snails.

7

HENRY PLANS THE BEST EVER BREAKFAST IN BED FOR HIS MUM ON MOTHER'S DAY. WHAT DOES SHE GET IN THE END?

a. Pizza, sweets, crisps and fizzywizz.

b. Two raw eggs and a glass of orange juice.

c. A bowl of Glop.

8

WHAT DOES MARGARET DO TO MAKE SURE HENRY DOESN'T WIN THE STREET PARTY BAKE-OFF COMPETITION?

a. She fills Henry's sugar jar with salt.

b. She stomps on Henry's cake until it's flat as a pancake.

c. She scoops out the middle of Henry's cake and fills it with ketchup.

CHECK YOUR SCORE ON PAGE 58.

HOW DID YOU DO?

9–10:

A lip-smacking top score! Your prize is a year's supply of Triple Choc Chip Marshmallow Chewies.

5–8:

A mouth-wateringly medium score. You win a lovely lopsided cupcake created by Perfect Peter for the street party bake-off competition.

0–4:

A gut-wrenchingly rotten score. Your punishment is a big bowl of Rotten Crispies and Nasty Nuts washed down by a bottle of Dungeon Drink. Yeuch!

HORRID HENRY EATS A VEGETABLE

"Ugggh! Gross! Yuck! Bleeeeeech!"

Horrid Henry glared at the horrible, disgusting food slithering on his plate. Globby slobby blobs. Bumpy lumps. Rubbery blubbery globules of glop. Ugghh!

How Dad and Mum and Peter could eat this swill without throwing up was amazing. Henry poked at the white, knobbly clump. It looked like brains. It felt like brains. Maybe it was … Ewwwwwwww. Horrid Henry pushed away his plate.

"I can't eat this," moaned Henry. "I'll be sick!"

"Henry! Cauliflower cheese is delicious," said Mum.

"And nutritious," said Dad.

"I love it," said Perfect Peter. "Can I have seconds?"

"It's nice to know someone appreciates my cooking," said Dad. He frowned at Henry.

"But I hate vegetables," said Henry. Yuck. Vegetables were so … healthy. And tasted so … vegetably. "I want pizza!"

"Well, you can't have it," said Dad.

"Ralph has pizza and chips every night at his house," said Henry. "And Graham never has to eat vegetables."

"I don't care what Ralph and Graham eat," said Mum.

"You've got to eat more vegetables," said Dad.

"I eat loads of vegetables," said Henry.

"Name one," said Dad.

"Crisps," said Henry.

"Crisps aren't vegetables, are they, Mum?" said Perfect Peter.

"No," said Mum. "Go on, Henry."

"Ketchup," said Henry.

"Ketchup is not a vegetable," said Dad.

"It's impossible cooking for you," said Mum.

"You're such a picky eater," said Dad.

"I eat loads of things," said Henry.

"Like what?" said Dad.

"Chips. Crisps. Burgers. Pizza. Chocolate. Sweets. Cake. Biscuits. Loads of food," said Horrid Henry.

"That's not very healthy, Henry," said Perfect Peter. "You haven't said any fruit or vegetables."

"So?" said Henry. "Mind your own business, Toad."

"Henry called me Toad," wailed Peter.

"Ribbet. Ribbet," croaked Horrid Henry.

"Don't be horrid, Henry," snapped Dad.

"You can't go on eating so unhealthily," said Mum.

"Agreed," said Dad.

Uh oh, thought Henry. Here it comes. Nag nag nag. If there were prizes for best naggers Mum would win every time.

"I'll make a deal with you, Henry," said Mum.

"What?" said Henry suspiciously. Mum and Dad's "deals" usually involved his doing something horrible, for a pathetic reward. Well no way was he falling for that again.

"If you eat all your vegetables for five nights in a row, we'll take you to Gobble and Go."

DOES HENRY BEAT THIS TOUGH CHALLENGE? FIND OUT IN 'HORRID HENRY EATS A VEGETABLE' FROM HORRID HENRY: UNDERPANTS PANIC

16

HORRID HENRY VS THE VICIOUS VEGETABLES

MUM AND DAD HAVE PROMISED TO TAKE ME TO GOBBLE AND GO IF I EAT ALL MY VEGETABLES FOR 5 DAYS. NO PROBLEM! ALL IT TAKES IS 5 VEG-TACKLING TACTICS . . .

1

I'll pretend to choke on the tiniest bite of veg – and beg and plead for water. While Dad fills the water jug, I'll shout that there's a spider under the table to distract Mum and Peter. Then, when no one's watching, I'll dump all my veg on to Peter's plate. Job done!

2

I'll drop my vegetables – by accident! – and quickly kick them under Peter's chair. Mum will be horrified when she sees what a mess he's made, hee hee!

3

I'll stuff my veg into the little drawer in the table in front of my chair. A perfect, Brussels sprout-sized drawer. While pretending to eat them all, of course!

4

I'll pretend a fly has landed on the veg, and rush to dump it all in the bin. After all, they can't possibly make me eat it now. Not after a filthy, horrible, disgusting fly has walked all over it, spreading germs and dirt and poo …

5

Top tactic for peas! I'll squish them one by one under my knife – then offer to clear the table and quickly rinse all the peas off my knife.

A FEW EVIL VEGETABLES CAN'T BEAT ME. GOBBLE AND GO – HERE I COME!!!!

PERFECT PETER'S PERFECT PUZZLE

PERFECT PETER HAS HIDDEN HIS FAVOURITE FRUIT AND VEGETABLES IN THIS WORDSEARCH PUZZLE. CAN YOU FIND THEM? LOOK UP, DOWN, BACKWARDS, FORWARDS AND DIAGONALLY.

APPLE

MELON

BANANA

STRAWBERRY

GRAPES

SPROUTS

CABBAGE

BEANS

CARROT

PEAS

BROCCOLI

SWEETCORN

S	P	I	C	G	B	K	L	E	S
D	W	O	N	A	R	E	I	T	O
S	N	E	N	M	G	A	R	O	N
N	P	A	E	A	E	A	P	O	S
T	N	R	B	T	W	L	L	E	B
A	O	B	O	B	C	E	P	E	S
T	A	R	E	U	M	O	A	P	S
C	E	R	R	R	T	N	R	M	A
U	R	N	C	A	S	S	H	N	E
Y	I	L	O	C	C	O	R	B	P

HORRID HENRY HAS SNEAKED ONE OF HIS FAVOURITE SNACKS INTO THE PUZZLE TOO. YOU CAN FIND IT BY WRITING THE LEFTOVER LETTERS INTO THE SPACES BELOW.

_ _ _ _ _ _ _   _ _ _ _ _   _ _ _ _ _ _ _   _ _ _ _ _

TANGLED SPAGHETTI

IT'S SPAGHETTI WITH MEATBALLS FOR TEA – HORRID HENRY'S FAVOURITE – AND THERE'S SOME LEFT OVER! FOLLOW THE TANGLED SPAGHETTI TO SEE WHO GETS THE SECONDS ...

CLEVER CLARE'S FUNNY FOOD

VIBRANT VEG

HENRY'S TIP:
Who wants to eat celery? Here's how to get rid of it all!

YOU WILL NEED:

- celery
- food colouring (concentrated gel)
- water
- jam jars or tall glasses
(as many as you like)

INSTRUCTIONS

1. Add water to each jar – to around three-quarters full.
2. Put around ten drops of food colouring in each jar.
3. Pop a stick of celery into each jar.
4. Leave the celery overnight – and check out the crazy colours in the morning!

CLEVER CLARE EXPLAINS:
THIS EXPERIMENT SHOWS HOW WATER MOVES UPWARDS THROUGH PLANTS.

JUMPING RAISINS

WHAT YOU NEED:

- a tall glass
- a few raisins
- fizzy lemonade or fizzy water

INSTRUCTIONS

1. Pour some fizzy drink into the glass.
2. Add a few raisins. Watch and wait!
3. After a few seconds, the raisins start jumping about in the glass.

CLEVER CLARE EXPLAINS: THE TINY BUBBLES IN THE FIZZY DRINK STICK TO THE RAISINS AND CARRY THEM UP TO THE TOP. ONCE THE BUBBLES START TO POP, THE RAISINS SINK BACK DOWN TO THE BOTTOM.

HENRY'S TIP:

Here's how to stop parents sneaking wrinkly, revolting raisins into your lunchbox.

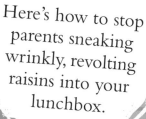

MAKE YOUR OWN BUTTER

YOU WILL NEED:

- whipping cream (any amount)
- jam jar with a tight lid

HENRY'S TIP:

Shaking is hot, heavy work. Find a parent or little brother to do it for you!

INSTRUCTIONS

1. Put the cream in the jar and screw the lid on tightly.
2. Shake the cream in the jar for about 15 minutes.
The cream gets thicker and thicker – but don't give up – keep on shaking!
3. Suddenly, you will see lots of liquid sloshing around in your jar.
Open the jar and you'll find a lump of butter.
4. Rinse your butter carefully under cold water.
You can eat your butter and it will keep in the fridge for two days.

WHAT TYPE OF FRUIT OR VEG ARE YOU?

ARE YOU A POTATO, AN ORANGE OR A PEA? FOLLOW THE FLOW CHART AND FIND OUT!

START

Do you like eating fruit and vegetables? — **YES** → Which colour do you like better – green or orange? — **ORANGE** → Are you top of the class at school?

I DUNNO → Are you a **TURNIP**, like **BEEFY BERT**? Who knows?

ONLY CHIPS → Are you kind to your younger brothers and sisters?

GREEN → Do you ever help out at home?

NEVER → Do you ever help out at home?

SOMETIMES / **YES** → Just like **CLEVER CLARE**, you're sharp and bright. You're an **ORANGE!**

You are a **BANANA!**

Are you kind to your younger brothers and sisters? — **NO** → Do you ever help out at home?

Do you ever help out at home? — **YES** → Do you do ALL your homework on time? — **NO** → Do you do ALL your homework on time?

Are you kind to your younger brothers and sisters? — **YES** → Are you long and yellow with an easy-to-peel skin? — **YES** → You are a **BANANA!**

Do you do ALL your homework on time? — **YES** → Is your bedroom neat and tidy?

Like **HORRID HENRY**, you like lazing around, and your favourite veg is chips! You're a **POTATO.**

Are you long and yellow with an easy-to-peel skin? — **NO** → Like **HORRID HENRY**...

Do you do ALL your homework on time? — **NO** → Do you love watching TV and eating crisps?

Is your bedroom neat and tidy? — **NO** → Do you love watching TV and eating crisps?

Are you long and yellow with an easy-to-peel skin? — **NO** → Do you like playing sport? — **YES** → Do you always want to be the leader?

Is your bedroom neat and tidy? — **YES** → Like **PERFECT PETER**, you're a sweet little **PEA.**

Do you like playing sport? — **HILARIOUS** → Like **SOUR SUSAN**, you're very sour. You're a a bitter **LEMON.**

Do you like playing sport? — **NO** → What's your best friend like? — **BOSSY** → Like **SOUR SUSAN**, you're very sour. You're a a bitter **LEMON.**

Do you always want to be the leader? — **YES** → Like **MOODY MARGARET**, you're so mean, you make people cry. You're an **ONION!**

Do you always want to be the leader? — **SOMETIMES** → You're long and lean like **Aerobic Al**. You're a cool **CUCUMBER!**

22

PYRAMID PICTURE CROSSWORD

CHECK OUT HORRID HENRY'S FOOD PYRAMID AND COMPLETE THE CROSSWORD!

CLUES

ACROSS
1. A holder for ice cream.
4. Henry loves this food with chips and ketchup.
6. Something for sucking up fizzy drinks.

DOWN
2. How many lollipops can you see?
3. These snacks are salty and crunchy.
4. One of the colours on the stripy bowl.
5. How many Gooey Chooeys can you count?
7. Two of the sweets are this bright colour.

MOODY MARGARET'S MAGNIFICENT MAKEOVER MIXTURES

HERE'S HOW MOODY MARGARET MAKES TWO OF HER BEST-SELLING MIRACLE MIXTURES.

SWEET PORRIDGE FACE PACK

YOU WILL NEED:

- ½ cup of hot water
- 4 tablespoons of oats
- 1 teaspoon of plain yogurt
- 1 teaspoon of runny honey
- 1 egg white

INSTRUCTIONS

1. Mix the hot water and oats together and leave for five minutes.
2. Mix in the yogurt, honey and egg white.
3. Sell this slop to someone mean and grumpy.

MUSHY MASK

YOU WILL NEED:

- 1 ripe banana
- 1 teaspoon of plain yogurt
- 1 teaspoon of runny honey

INSTRUCTIONS

1. Mash up the banana with a fork.
2. Stir in the yogurt and honey. All done!
3. Sell the mush for lots of money to someone rich, old and ugly.

MARGARET'S TIP:

This sweet face pack is specially made for mean old grumps, like Sour Susan.

HOW TO USE BOTH MAKEOVER MIXTURES:

Smear the gunk all over your face, relax for 10 minutes, and wash it all off with warm water.

SPOT THE DIFFERENCE

HORRID HENRY IS SWAPPING THE LUNCHBOX SNACKS!
LOOK CAREFULLY AT THE LUNCHES ON THIS PAGE. THEN
TURN TO PAGE 26 AND SEE IF YOU CAN WORK
OUT WHAT HENRY HAS TAKEN FROM EACH OF THEM.
TRY NOT TO PEEK BACK AT THIS PAGE!

CAN YOU WORK OUT WHICH ITEMS HENRY HAS REMOVED?

LUNCHBOX 1 _____

LUNCHBOX 2 _____

LUNCHBOX 3 _____

LUNCHBOX 4 _____

WORD GAMES

SPLIT WORDS

CAN YOU MATCH UP THESE SPLIT WORDS TO MAKE 8 TYPES OF FOOD?

1. straw _____   a. room
2. ketch _____   b. ball
3. marsh _____   c. rot
4. car _____   d. nut
5. mush _____   e. up
6. pop _____   f. berry
7. dough _____   g. corn
8. meat _____   h. mallow

DUNGEON DRINK MUDDLED-UP WORDS

UNTANGLE THE WORDS AND FIND OUT WHAT HENRY IS BREWING IN HIS DUNGEON DRINK.

1. upso   _ _ _ _ _
2. acol   _ _ _ _ _
3. cijue   _ _ _ _ _ _
4. hillic _ _ _ _ _ _ _
5. rugtoy _ _ _ _ _ _ _

THE LAWS OF KING HENRY THE HORRIBLE

I, KING HENRY THE HORRIBLE, HEREBY BAN THESE REVOLTING FOODS, BY ROYAL LAW:

1) CAULIFLOWER CHEESE, SPROUTS, APPLES AND ALL OTHER FRUIT, VEGCHUP (THIS IS NOT KETCHUP), MUESLI, SALAD.

PARENTS SHOULD GIVE CHILDREN THE FOOD THEY LIKE – EVERY DAY.

TEACHERS ARE FORCED TO EAT SCHOOL DINNERS.

ONLY CHILDREN WHO CAN'T SPELL ARE REWARDED WITH SWEETS.

BEASTLY BABYSITTERS LIKE RABID REBECCA WILL BE CATAPULTED INTO THE MOAT AND FED TO MY ROYAL PIRANHA FISH.

DRESSING UP AS VEGETABLES AND DANCING IS BANNED. (DANCE CLASS WITH MISS IMPATIENCE TUTU IS BANNED FOR EVER.)

THESE ARE THE ROYAL LAWS AND ANYONE WHO BREAKS THEM WILL BE PUNISHED ...

ANYONE NAMED MARGARET WILL BE BOILED IN OIL AND FED TO THE CROWS.

ENEMIES OF THE KING TO BE IMPRISONED WITHOUT FOOD

EVIL ENEMIES LIKE STUCK-UP STEVE AND BOSSY BILL SHOULD BE FED TO SNAKES AND SHARKS.

THE KING SHALL BE SERVED A ROYAL BANQUET EVERY DAY.

CHILDREN SHALL HENCEFORTH EAT SWEETS INSTEAD OF SCHOOL DINNERS OR GO TO GOBBLE AND GO.

KING HENRY'S BRILLIANT BANQUET

CRISPS SERVED ON A SILVER PLATTER
ROYAL BURGER AND CHIPS
POSH PIZZA
THE KING'S KETCHUP

29

TRUE OR FALSE?

CHECK OUT THE 10 FOOD FACTS BELOW. ARE THEY TRUE OR FALSE? YOU DECIDE!

2

CUCUMBERS AND TOMATOES ARE FRUIT, NOT VEGETABLES.

TRUE? ☐
FALSE? ☐

1

VOMIT OFTEN LOOKS LIKE CHOPPED UP CARROTS BECAUSE THE ORANGE STUFF IS PART OF YOUR STOMACH LINING.

TRUE? ☐   FALSE? ☐

3

EATING BREAD CRUSTS MAKES YOUR HAIR CURLY.

TRUE? ☐   FALSE? ☐

4

IF YOU DROP YOUR TOAST, IT ALWAYS LANDS BUTTERED SIDE DOWN.

TRUE? ☐
FALSE? ☐

5

LEMONS CONTAIN MORE SUGAR THAN STRAWBERRIES.

TRUE? ☐   FALSE? ☐

6

IN JAPAN AND CHINA, GRASSHOPPERS ARE FRIED AND SERVED WITH RICE.

TRUE? ☐
FALSE? ☐

7

EATING PIZZA EVERY DAY MAKES YOU CLEVER.

TRUE? ☐ FALSE? ☐

9

TRIPE IS A TYPE OF FISH.

TRUE? ☐
FALSE? ☐

8

IT TAKES AROUND FOUR HOURS TO HARD-BOIL AN OSTRICH EGG.

TRUE? ☐ FALSE? ☐

10

BLACK PUDDING IS MADE OF LIQUORICE.

TRUE? ☐
FALSE? ☐

CHECK YOUR SCORE ON PAGE 58.
HOW DID YOU DO?

7–10

Fantastic! A fabulous fib-busting score!

4–6

Perfectly pathetic! Even puny pantsface Perfect Peter scored more than that!

0–3

That's bad! Beefy Bert scored zero – did you beat him?

CHEESY CHILLI POWDER BISCUITS

WHEN GREASY GRETA SNEAKS THE KIDS' GOODIES, HORRID HENRY PLANS THE PERFECT REVENGE – TREATS THAT AREN'T AS TASTY AS THEY LOOK! YOU CAN DO THIS TOO BY MAKING THESE CHEESY BISCUITS NICE OR NASTY!

WHAT YOU NEED:

- 120 grams of plain flour
- 120 grams of butter
- 120 grams of cheddar cheese, grated
- rolling pin
- biscuit cutter
- non-stick baking tray
- adult to help
- chilli powder (optional!)

INSTRUCTIONS

1. Ask your adult to preheat the oven to 170°C or Gas Mark 5.

2. Using your fingers, rub the flour and butter together in a big bowl.

3. Mix in the cheese with your hands until you have a sticky dough.

4. Roll out the dough on a well-floured board to a thickness of around 5mm.

5. Cut out the biscuits with your biscuit cutter.

6. Place the biscuits on a non-stick baking tray, and ask your adult to bake them in the oven for about 20 minutes before cooling on a wire tray.

CHILLI BISCUITS

If you want to spike a few of your biscuits with chilli and play Henry's game, save a handful of the dough till last. Sprinkle on a little chilli powder, blend it in; then roll out and bake with the other biscuits.

HENRY'S CHILLI GAME

Hand round a plate of your cheesy biscuits. But beware – one of these tasty treats is spiked with hot chilli powder, and one unlucky person is in for a nasty surprise!

HORRID HENRY AND THE REVENGE OF THE DEMON DINNER LADY

"We've decided to appoint a lunchbox monitor, who will be checking every day and confiscating all unhealthy snacks," said Mrs Oddbod. "From today we will be a sweet-free school."

Huh?

Horrid Henry sat up. This did not sound good. In fact, this sounded TERRIBLE.

"I'm delighted to welcome back an old friend to our school, someone who has been sorely missed. Children, please say hello to our new healthy food monitor – Greta!"

An enormous woman stood up and waddled over to Mrs Oddbod. Horrid Henry's blood turned to ice. It wasn't – it couldn't be –

Greta. Greasy Greta. Greasy Greta, the Demon Dinner Lady! That ape in an apron, that demon in dungarees, that sneaky sweet-snatcher, that gobbling treat-grabber. The last time Henry had seen Greta she'd run howling out of school after he'd spiked some biscuits with hot chilli powder. And now she was back … bigger and meaner and more demonic than ever.

Greasy Greta, a healthy food monitor? She'd grab all the treats for herself, and leave the carrots and celery sticks and wholemeal bread behind. No one could sniff out sweets faster than Greasy Greta.

"I'll be checking all lunchboxes very thoroughly," said Greasy Greta. "Very, very thoroughly. No sneaky sweets will escape me."

"Are there any questions?" said Mrs Oddbod.

Greedy Graham's hand shot up.

"What's going to happen to all the sweets?" he asked.

"All confiscated sweets will be given to charity," said Mrs Oddbod.

"That's right," said Greta. "All confiscated sweets will be safely disposed of." And she smiled her horrible greasy smile and flashed her mouldy teeth.

Yeah, down her gob, thought Henry mournfully. What a job. Like putting a fox in charge of the rabbit hutches.

"Greta will also be giving healthy-eating talks," said Mrs Oddbod.

"Sweets are bad for you," said Greta. "I never touch them. Eat vegetables."

What a liar, thought Horrid Henry. I'll bet she's never eaten a vegetable in her life.

But what to do? What to do? He couldn't face school lunches with Sloppy Sally sloshing food all over his tray. He wanted to keep his packed lunch AND all his treats. But how? How? Somehow he'd have to find a way …

DOES HENRY FIND A WAY TO OUTWIT GREASY GRETA? AND WHAT HAPPENS TO ALL THE SWEETS? FIND OUT IN 'REVENGE OF THE DEMON DINNER LADY' FROM HORRID HENRY: NIGHTMARE!

33

START

START

START

START

34

THE GIZMO GAME

RACE TO SEE WHO CAN COLLECT ALL TEN GIZMOS FIRST!

WHAT YOU NEED:

- 2 or more players
- pencils
- dice
- counters – a different colour counter for each player

INSTRUCTIONS

1. Choose a start square. Take it in turns to throw the dice and move around the board on the white paths. You can move in any direction – but only in one direction each turn.

2. Whenever you land on a GIZMO square at the end of your go, tick the matching GIZMO on your list.

5. The first player to collect all the GIZMOs is the winner.

START

COPY THE LIST BELOW TO MAKE YOUR GIZMO TICK LIST.

35

GROOVY GRUB GAMES

GAMES TO PLAY WITH YOUR FAMILY AND FRIENDS.

FLOURY FACE FUN

WHAT YOU NEED:

- one chocolate button
- flour
- pudding basin
- large plate
- blunt knife
- dice

HENRY'S TIP:
Scoff the rest of the chocolate buttons when no one's looking, tee hee!

HOW TO PREPARE

1. Fill the pudding basin with flour, pressing it down hard. Put the plate on top of the basin, then quickly turn it over so that you have a firm mound of flour on the plate.
2. Pop a chocolate button on top of the mound.

HOW TO PLAY

1. Sit in a circle around the mound of flour.
2. Take it in turns to throw the dice. If you throw a six, go to the middle of the circle, and use the knife to slice off a section of the flour. The aim is NOT to make the chocolate button topple off the top of the mound.
3. The first person who makes the chocolate button fall off the flour has to pick up the chocolate using only their mouth.

CHOCOLATE BLOWING

WHAT YOU NEED

- chocolate malt balls
- straws

HOW TO PLAY

Have a race by blowing the chocolate malt balls along the floor using straws. Anyone caught pushing the chocolate balls instead of blowing is disqualified for cheating. If anyone scoffs the chocolates, the game is over!

CHOPPING THE CHOCOLATE

WHAT YOU NEED

- wooden board
- bar of chocolate
- fork and blunt knife
- hat, scarf and gloves
- dice

HOW TO PREPARE

Place the bar of chocolate on the wooden board, with the fork and knife.

GLOP GAME

HOW TO PLAY

1. The first player says: I made some Glop and I added … **a worm** (for example – but you can add anything you like!)
2. The second player says: I made some Glop and I added … **a worm** … and **some porridge**.
3. Each player needs to remember what has already been added – in order – and then add a new ingredient. Players are knocked out if they forget anything on the list or muddle up the order.
4. The winner is the player who keeps going the longest.

HOW TO PLAY

1. Sit in a circle around the chocolate.
2. Take it in turns to throw the dice. If you throw a six, run to the middle of the circle and quickly put on the hat, scarf and gloves. Try to eat as much of the chocolate as you can, using only the knife and fork.
3. While you are doing this, the other players continue to throw the dice. As soon as someone else throws a six, your go is over, so you pull off the hat, scarf and gloves and return to your place.
4. The game is over when all the chocolate has been chomped!

SECRET CLUB COOKIE MAZE

HELP HORRID HENRY SNEAK THE SECRET CLUB'S STASH OF COOKIES.
IF YOU REACH A DAGGER – BAD LUCK – YOU'VE HIT A DEAD END!

MOODY MARGARET'S MEALTIME RULES

MY VERY VERY IMPORTANT RULES!!

- NO BAKED BEANS.

- NO SALT.

- THE VEGETABLES SHOULD ALWAYS BE PEAS.

- VEGETABLES SHOULD BE ON A SEPARATE PLATE.

- DO NOT BREAK MY EGG YOLK. IF YOU DO, START AGAIN.

- SUPPER IS AT SIX O'CLOCK AND NOT A MINUTE LATER.

- NO CORN ON THE COB. IT HAS TO BE CORN OFF THE COB.

- VEGETABLES SHOULD NEVER TOUCH THE MEAT.

- BREAKFAST IS AT HALF PAST SIX, IMMEDIATELY AFTER I'VE PRACTISED MY TRUMPET.

CAN YOU GUESS WHO SAID WHAT ABOUT MOODY MARGARET?			
	Her mum and dad	Horrid Henry	Do you agree? YES or NO?
She is ALWAYS polite			
She eats EVERYTHING			
She is a grumpy frogface			
She NEVER complains			
She is a bossyboots grouch			
She is the world's most horrible girl			

MATCH THE PAIRS

PERFECT PETER TRIES TO BE HORRID ONE DAY, AND HE TAKES A BITE OUT OF ALL OF GRANDMA'S CHOCOLATES! HERE ARE EIGHT PAIRS OF CHOCS – CAN YOU MATCH THEM UP?

A   B   C   D

E   F   G   H

I   J   K   L

M   N   O   P

THE MATCHING PAIRS ARE: ___ and ___   ___ and ___   ___ and ___

___ and ___   ___ and ___   ___ and ___

___ and ___   ___ and ___

41

JOLLY JOKES DOUBLE PUZZLE

CAN YOU FIT THE FOLLOWING WORDS INTO THE CRISS-CROSS PUZZLE?

4 LETTERS
- half
- hill
- soup
- eggs

5 LETTERS
- teeth
- bites
- smell
- cream
- bunny
- green

6 LETTERS
- grapes
- beaten

7 LETTERS
- peeling

HENRY'S TIP:
Beware of the 5-letter words!

NOW SEE IF YOU CAN WORK OUT WHICH OF THE CRISS-CROSS PUZZLE WORDS ARE MISSING TO COMPLETE THE JOKES ON THIS PAGE ...

1. WHAT'S WORSE THAN FINDING A WORM IN YOUR APPLE?

Finding _ _ _ _ _ a worm in your apple!

2. WHY DID THE BOILED EGG WIN THE RACE?

It couldn't be

_ _ _ _ _ _ .

3. WHY IS A TOMATO ROUND AND RED?

Because if it was long and _ _ _ _ _ _ it would be a cucumber.

4. WHY WAS THE PACKED LUNCH SO STINKY?

It had passed its _ _ _ _ _ _ -by date.

5. HOW DO YOU MAKE A SAUSAGE ROLL?

Push it down a _ _ _ _ _ .

6. WHY DID THE BANANA GO TO THE DOCTOR?

Because it wasn't _ _ _ _ _ _ _ _ _ very well.

7. WHY ARE COOKS MEAN?

Because they beat the _ _ _ _ _ _ and whip the _ _ _ _ _ _ .

8. WHAT'S THE BEST THING TO PUT INTO A SANDWICH?

Your _ _ _ _ _ !

HORRID HENRY AND THE NUDIE FOODIE

"A healthy school is a happy school," said Mr Nudie Foodie, beaming. "My motto is: Only bad food boos, when you choose yummy food. And at lunchtime today, all your parents will be coming to the cafeteria to sample our scrumptious, yummalicious, fabulicious and irresistible new food! Olé!"

Horrid Henry looked round the school kitchen. He'd never seen so many pots and pans and vats and cauldrons. So this was where the school glop was made. Well, not any longer. Would they be making giant whopper burgers in the huge frying pans? Or vats and vats of chips in the huge pots? Maybe they'd make pizzas for the gigantic ovens!

The Nudie Foodie stood before Henry's class. "This is so exciting," he said, bouncing up and down. "Everyone ready to make some delicious food?"

"Yes!" bellowed Henry's class.

"Right, then, let's get cooking," said Mr Nudie Foodie.

Horrid Henry stood in front of a chopping board with Weeping William, Dizzy Dave and Fiery Fiona. Fiery Fiona shoved Henry.

"Stop hogging the chopping board," she hissed.

Horrid Henry shoved her back, knocking the lumpy bag of ingredients on to the floor.

"Stop hogging it yourself," he hissed back.

"Wah!" wailed Weepy William. "Henry pushed me."

Wait. What was rolling all over the floor? It looked like … it couldn't be … "Group 1, here's how to slice a yummy green pepper," beamed Mr Nudie Foodie. "And Group 2, you're in charge of the tomatoes … Group 3, you make the broccoli salad. Group 4 will look after the mushrooms."

Green pepper? Tomatoes? Broccoli? Mushrooms? What was this muck?

"It's my yummy, scrummy, super, secret, vege-tastic pasta sauce!" said Mr Nudie Foodie.

What? What a dirty rotten trick. Where were the chips? Where were the burgers?

And then suddenly Horrid Henry understood Mr Nudie Foodie's evil plan. He was going to sneak vegetables on to the school menu. Not just a single vegetable, but loads and loads and loads of vegetables. Enough evil vegetables to kill someone a hundred times over. *Boy impaled by killer carrot. Girl chokes to death on deadly broccoli. Boy gags on toxic tomato.* Henry could see the headlines now. They'd find him dead in the lunchroom, poisoned by vegetables, his limbs twisted in agony …

Well, no way. No way was this foul fiend going to trick Henry into eating vegetables.

DOES HENRY FOIL MR NUDIE FOODIE AND HIS FOUL FOOD? FIND OUT IN 'HORRID HENRY AND THE NUDIE FOODIE' FROM *HORRID HENRY: ZOMBIE VAMPIRE.*

SECRET SAUCE

HENRY THROWS SALT, MUSTARD, VINEGAR OR LARD INTO THE FOUR VATS OF THE NUDIE FOODIE'S VEGETABLE SAUCE WHEN NO ONE'S LOOKING.

WORK OUT WHICH INGREDIENT HE PUTS IN THE VATS BELOW. CROSS OUT ANY LETTER THAT APPEARS TWICE, AND THEN UNTANGLE THE LEFTOVER LETTERS.

LEFTOVER LETTERS

_____

_____

ANSWER

_____

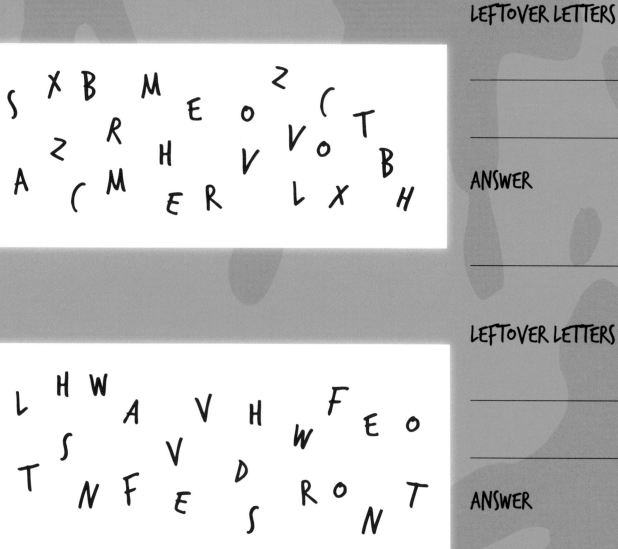

LEFTOVER LETTERS

_____

_____

ANSWER

_____

WHAT'S IN THE GLOP?

HORRID HENRY AND MOODY MARGARET MAKE THE YUCKIEST GLOP EVER. UNCODE THE LIST BELOW TO WORK OUT WHAT THEY ADDED TO THEIR GLOP, USING THE GLOP CODE GRID.

GLOP CODE GRID

TO USE THE CODE GRID, FIND THE LETTER YOU WANT TO USE IN THE WHITE SQUARES. TO PUT IT INTO CODE, USE THE YELLOW LETTER ALONG THE SIDE, FOLLOWED BY THE YELLOW NUMBER ALONG THE TOP.

SO: A = A5, B = B1, C = B2 ...

	1	2	3	4	5
A	G	L	O	P	A
B	B	C	D	E	F
C	H	I	J	K	M
D	N	Q	R	S	T
E	U	V	W	X	Y

UNTANGLE THE GLOP LIST!

c5 a3 e1 a2 b3 e5   b2 c1 b4 b4 d4 b4 _____

d4 a4 c2 d1 a5 b2 c1 _____

d3 a3 d5 d5 b4 d1   a3 d3 a5 d1 a1 b4 d4 _____

a4 a3 d3 d3 c2 b3 a1 b4 _____

e2 c2 d1 b4 a1 a5 d3 _____

c5 e1 d4 d5 a5 d3 b3 _____

CAN YOU ADD A COUPLE OF SECRET INGREDIENTS USING GLOP CODE?

_____

GLOP PUDDING

GLOP ALWAYS LOOKS GRUESOME, BUT IT CAN TASTE DELICIOUS! TRY MAKING THIS WORMY PUDDING . . .

YOU WILL NEED:

- creamy chocolate desserts
- sweets, nuts and chocolates (your choice)
- chocolate biscuits
- gummy worms
- plastic bag
- rolling pin
- big bowl
- individual bowls for serving

INSTRUCTIONS

1. Put your creamy chocolate desserts into the big bowl.
2. Throw any sweets, nuts or chocolates you have into the bowl – and mix up to make gloppy goo!
3. Divide the Glop into the individual bowls.
4. Put some chocolate biscuits into the plastic bag and bash with the rolling pin.
5. Sprinkle biscuit crumbs on top of the Glop.
6. Place two or three gummy worms on top of the crumbs. You're done! Now dare your friends and family to eat Glop pudding!

THE BIG BAKE WORDSEARCH

CAN YOU FIND ALL THESE TASTY BAKES, CAKES AND COOKIES IN THE WORDSEARCH?
LOOK UP, DOWN, BACKWARDS, FORWARDS AND DIAGONALLY.

- CHOCOLATE
- PARKIN
- LEMON
- BROWNIE
- MUFFIN
- GINGERBREAD
- MACAROON
- FLAPJACK
- WAFER
- DOUGHNUT
- CUPCAKE
- BUN
- ÉCLAIR
- SPONGE
- SCONE
- TART
- BAGEL

S	B	Q	K	W	A	F	E	R	G	N
E	U	U	C	O	V	K	N	D	I	I
G	N	M	A	C	A	R	O	O	N	F
N	K	Z	J	C	R	P	C	U	G	F
O	O	U	P	I	E	N	S	G	E	U
P	O	U	A	I	I	O	D	H	R	M
S	C	L	L	J	N	M	B	N	B	T
G	C	X	F	Z	W	E	F	U	R	A
E	C	H	O	C	O	L	A	T	E	R
B	R	N	I	K	R	A	P	O	A	T
L	E	G	A	B	B	N	S	X	D	O

COLOUR HENRY

COLOUR IN THIS STINKY PICTURE OF HENRY USING YOUR FAVOURITE COLOURS!

DRAW YOUR OWN GREAT GRUB

CAN YOU DRAW YOUR OWN GREAT GRUB AND NIGHTMARE NOSH ON THE PLATES BELOW?

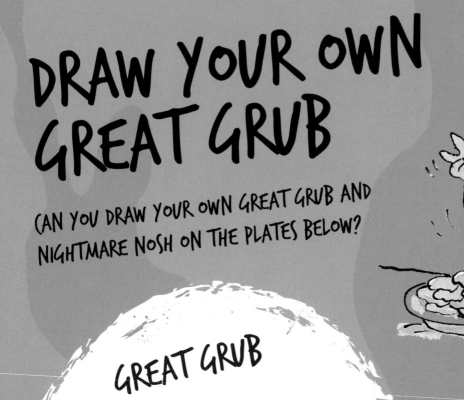

GREAT GRUB

NIGHTMARE NOSH

BUILD THE TALLEST TOWER

YOU WILL NEED:

- a packet of dried spaghetti
- a big bag of marshmallows
- a tray or board to build your tower on

INSTRUCTIONS

1. Start with a strong base.
2. Use the marshmallows as the joints between your pieces of spaghetti.
3. Push the spaghetti deep into the marshmallows to make it as strong as possible.
4. Always use two strands of spaghetti together.
5. Break the spaghetti into smaller pieces if you want.
6. Create your own amazing tower – and build it up as high as you can!

TOWER TOURNAMENT!

Hold a contest with your friends and compete to build the tallest tower in ten minutes!

WHO WANTS TO WORK FOR CHEF HENRY?

HORRID HENRY WANTS TO BE A CHEF WHEN HE GROWS UP AND OPEN A CHAIN OF RESTAURANTS CALLED "HENRY'S! WHERE THE EATIN' CAN'T BE BEATEN!" TRY THE QUIZ TO FIND OUT IF CHEF HENRY WOULD OFFER YOU A JOB . . .

1

HAVE YOU EVER WORKED FOR A TOP CHEF LIKE ME BEFORE?

a. I always help my parents when they are making tea – by setting the table and clearing up after.
b. No! I'm always the boss.
c. You're not a top chef. You're rubbish!

2

DO YOU HAVE ANY SPECIAL SKILLS?

a. I'm clean, tidy and polite.
b. I'm bossy and I make all the rules.
c. I'm brilliant at burping!

3

HOW WOULD YOU DESCRIBE SCHOOL DINNERS?

a. Delicious. Especially the lovely spinach salads.
b. Too much salt! Vegetables touching the meat. Disgusting!
c. Ugghhh! Yeuch! Horrible!

4

WHAT'S THE BEST THING YOU'VE EVER COOKED?

a. I made some lovely cupcakes. (Mum said they were perfect.)
b. Glop! It's delicious! Would you like to try it … ?
c. Cooking is for toady big bottoms!

5

HOW WOULD YOU ENCOURAGE PEOPLE TO COME TO THE RESTAURANT?

a. I'd walk the streets with a billboard and tell everyone how wonderful the restaurant is.

b. I'd order all my family and friends to go – or else!

c. I'd tell everyone about our food fights.

6

WHAT IS YOUR FAVOURITE COOKING PROGRAMME ON TV?

a. Cooking Cuties. I love finding out how to make my own muesli.

b. I don't watch cooking programmes. I already know how to cook.

c. The show with the most revolting food ever – CANNIBAL COOK!

7

IF I SHOUTED AT YOU AT WORK, WHAT WOULD YOU DO?

a. I'd tell Mum and Dad. It's horrid to shout.

b. I'd SCREAM!

c. I'd call you lots of rude names.

8

HOW WOULD YOU MAKE MY RESTAURANTS EVEN BETTER?

a. Add some healthy nutritious vegetables to the menu, turn off the loud music and invite someone to come and play the cello to the guests.

b. Get a better boss – and that would be ME!

c. Hold a burping competition every night!

DID YOU DO WELL IN YOUR INTERVIEW? FIND OUT BELOW.

MOSTLY As:

You're a pathetic worm, just like Perfect Peter. OK, I'll allow you to work in my fantastic brilliant restaurant – doing all the washing up, ha ha!!

MOSTLY Bs:

You're a bossyboots pants face, like Moody Margaret, and the worst person I've ever interviewed! But I'll let you work for me – scrubbing the kitchen floor – nah nah ne ne nah!

MOSTLY Cs:

Well done and welcome to my team! You sound really rude – like my best friend Rude Ralph – and loads of fun. Can you start straight away? BURP!!!!

53

TOP SECRET TRICKS

HORRID HENRY HAS LOTS OF SNEAKY TRICKS FOR SNEAKING SWEETS AND SNACKS . . . BUT THEY ARE ALL TOP SECRET . . . SO SHHHHH . . . DON'T TELL ANYONE!!!

FAKE ILLNESS

Pretending that my chest hurts, my head hurts and my throat hurts, works every time. I'm soon snuggled up in bed, watching TV, with Mum and Dad bringing me chocolate ice cream to soothe my poor throat.

PRETEND TO DO YOUR HOMEWORK

Miss Battle-Axe hands out a pack of Big Bopper sweets to everyone who spells all their words correctly in the test. But why go through the horrid hassle of learning to spell ... when I can copy off Clever Clare and still get the goodies, tee hee!

SNEAK THE SECRET CLUB'S STASH

If I sneak to the Secret Club tent when no one's around, I can always find Margaret's Secret Club biscuit tin, in her pathetic hiding place under a blanket. Is there anything more delicious in the whole wide world than a mouthful of nicked biscuits?

OUTWIT THE BABYSITTER

This is a perfect ploy when the babysitter is terrified of spiders. I simply pop a spider in a jar and threaten the babysitter with it unless she hides in the bathroom and doesn't come out. Then I can feast on all the ice cream and sweets and biscuits and crisps that my parents have left out for the babysitter!

TRICK PERFECT PETER

My game – Robot and Mad Professor – is a brilliant invention. I play the robot and Peter is the professor. In my best robotic voice, I demand sweets and money from the professor to prevent my batteries running down. Peter the professor hands over all his sweets and pocket money. I'm a genius!

SNEAK PERFECT PETER'S GRUMP CARDS

If I own a Grump Card, Mum and Dad can't be cross with me, whatever I do. I get away with scoffing every sweet, biscuit and treat in the house. But I never have a Grump Card, and Peter has loads. Luckily Peter will hand over his cards if I play with him – what a worm! With a Grump Card in my pocket, I can grab a huge handful of sweets from the jar – and if Mum starts screaming, "Put those back!" – I can whip out my grump card. Nah nah ne nah nah!

SCOFF ALL THE PRIZES

Organising my own Olympics with chocolate-chomping competitions and crisp-eating competitions – and getting everyone to pay to compete! It was a brilliant plan. Once I'd bought all the prizes, there was a whole heap of chocolate just sitting there for me to do my speed-eating practice!

SWEETIE SUDOKUS

FILL IN THE SUDOKUS SO THAT EVERY SQUARE, ROW AND COLUMN CONTAINS A RED, BLUE, YELLOW AND GREEN SWEET.

NOW TRY A TRICKIER ONE! FILL IN EVERY SQUARE, ROW AND COLUMN WITH NUMBERS 1-6.

	4	2		6	3
			5		
2	1			3	6
4		3		1	5
1				2	
	2				

ANSWERS!

THERE ARE 4 HIDDEN CHOCOLATE BARS.
PAGES: 20, 24, 31 AND 42

BRAINY BRIAN'S BIG QUIZ

1. A
2. B
3. B
4. C
5. A
6. C
7. B
8. A

TANGLED SPAGHETTI

MUM AND DAD GET THE SECONDS OF SPAGHETTI AND MEATBALLS.

PETER'S PERFECT PUZZLE

S	P	I	C	G	B	K	L	E	S
D	W	O	N	A	R	E	I	T	O
S	N	E	N	M	G	A	R	O	N
N	P	A	E	A	E	A	P	O	S
T	N	R	B	T	W	L	L	E	B
A	O	B	O	B	C	E	P	E	S
T	A	R	E	U	M	O	A	P	S
C	E	R	R	R	T	N	R	M	A
U	R	N	C	A	S	S	H	N	E
Y	I	L	O	C	C	O	R	B	P

THE LEFTOVER LETTERS SPELL OUT:
PICKLED ONION MONSTER MUNCH

PYRAMID PICTURE CROSSWORD

			¹C	²O	N	E
		³C		N		
⁴B	U	R	G	E	R	
L		I				⁵T
U		⁶S	T	⁷R	A	W
E		P		E		O
		S		D		

SECRET SAUCE

1. SALT   2. LARD

SPOT THE DIFFERENCE

1. FISH AND CHIPS
2. MUG OF TEA
3. PIZZA
4. FRUIT

WORD GAMES

THE SPLIT WORDS ARE:
1. STRAWBERRY
2. KETCHUP
3. MARSHMALLOW
4. CARROT
5. MUSHROOM
6. POPCORN
7. DOUGHNUT
8. MEATBALL

THE MUDDLED-UP WORDS ARE:
1. SOUP
2. COLA
3. JUICE
4. CHILLI
5. YOGURT

TRUE OR FALSE

1. TRUE
2. TRUE
3. FALSE: THERE IS NO PROOF THAT THIS IS TRUE.
4. FALSE: IT DEPENDS ON HOW YOU DROP YOUR TOAST, WHERE YOU DROP IT FROM AND HOW BIG YOUR TOAST IS!
5. TRUE
6. TRUE
7. FALSE: HORRID HENRY INVENTED THIS FACT!
8. TRUE
9. FALSE: TRIPE IS THE LINING OF A COW'S STOMACH.
10. FALSE: BLACK PUDDING IS MADE FROM PIG'S BLOOD AND OATS.

MATCH THE PAIRS

A AND K	D AND L	E AND O
B AND N	I AND J	H AND M
C AND F	G AND P	

THE BIG BAKE WORDSEARCH

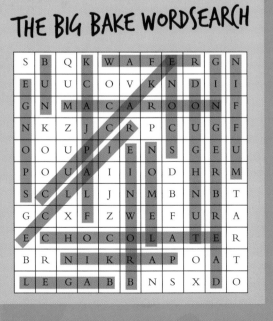

S	B	Q	K	W	A	F	E	R	G	N
E	U	U	C	O	V	K	N	D	I	I
G	N	M	A	C	A	R	O	O	N	F
N	K	Z	J	C	R	P	C	U	G	F
O	O	U	P	I	E	N	S	G	E	U
P	O	U	A	I	I	O	D	H	R	M
S	C	L	L	J	N	M	B	N	B	T
G	C	X	F	Z	W	E	F	U	R	A
E	C	H	O	C	O	L	A	T	E	T
B	R	N	I	K	R	A	P	O	A	T
L	E	G	A	B	B	N	S	X	D	O

SECRET CLUB COOKIE MAZE

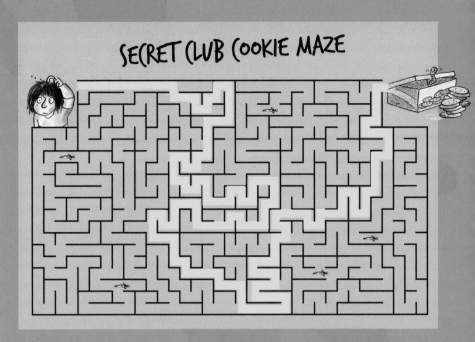

JOLLY JOKES DOUBLE PUZZLE

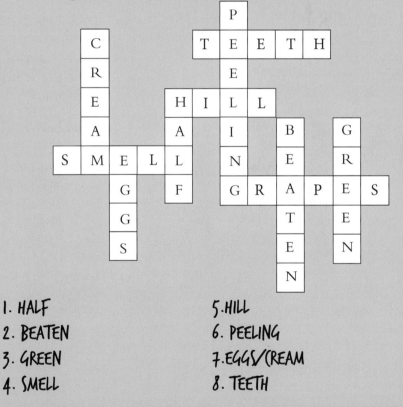

1. HALF		5. HILL
2. BEATEN		6. PEELING
3. GREEN		7. EGGS/CREAM
4. SMELL		8. TEETH

SWEETIE SUDOKUS

5	4	2	1	6	3
6	3	1	5	4	2
2	1	5	4	3	6
4	6	3	2	1	5
1	5	6	3	2	4
3	2	4	6	5	1

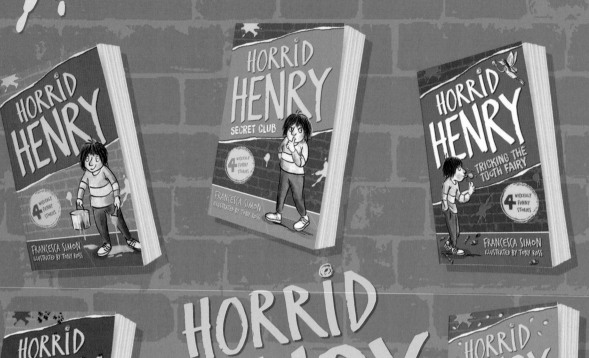

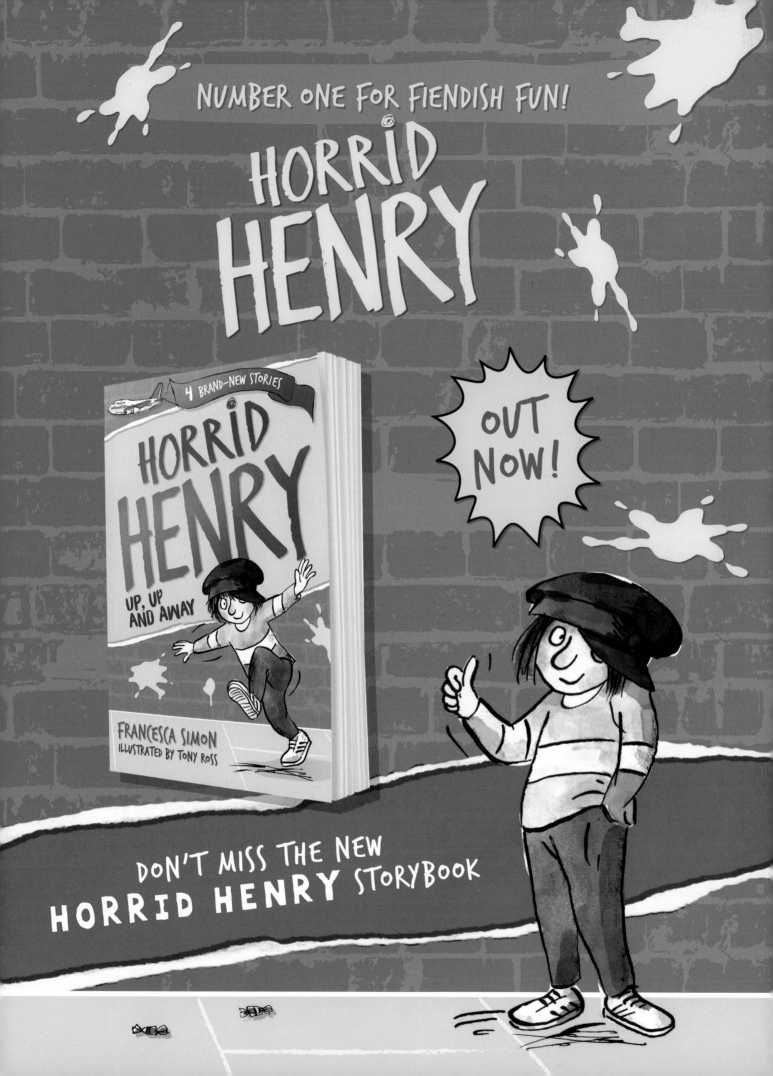